I Have A Dream Also!

Written by
Dwight F. Johnson Sr.

Illustrated by
Zipporah Cunningham

To order additional copies of this book, contact:
Xlibris
844-714-8691
www.Xlibris.com
Orders@Xlibris.com

ISBN: Softcover   978-1-6698-0378-2
       Hardcover   978-1-6698-0379-9
       EBook   978-1-6698-0377-5

Print information available on the last page.

Rev. date: 12/10/2021

I Have A Dream Also

The Dream

RAY RAY CRYSTAL KIM DREAM KING

King Team

ROSEY

FRANKIE

JOJO

I have a dream also,
that the dream of
Martin Luther King Jr.
will never grow old.

You should have a dream also,
and that's keeping our
children in the know!

Because of Dr. King's courageous
march on Washington and
all those who took action,
we now have affirmative action!

Yes, let's keep Dr. King's dream alive.

Not only did he give his life
;but many other people died.
Dr. King's dream was not only for
the black man; but for all mankind.

a dream also!

This memorial of a great man of God came with blood, sweat, and tears, to keep us from living in constant fear; so let's keep Dr. King's dream alive.

Yes, as a nation,
we should have a dream also;
for as we all know this great man
of God was taken from his family,
So let us continue to strive for
his goal, united as a family and
a nation with the same goal.

For united we stand
and divided we fall,
Dr. Martin Luther King
died for us all!

That's why God gave us a man of God,
so never let his dream die,
and let us keep
Dr. Martin Luther King's dream alive.

Do you have a dream also?

Printed in the United States
by Baker & Taylor Publisher Services